Bubbies-Babies

Created by
G. Brooks

Illustrated by
Mike Goldstein

www.Bubbies-Babies.com

Published by Black Cherry Publishing
bubbies-babies.com

Illustrated by Mike Goldstein

First Edition: November 2017

ISBN 978-0-9995516-0-8

Thank You, for making a difference!
For every book sold, Bubbies-Babies will make
a charitable donation to various organizations.

Bubbie's Quote of the Day

You are what makes the world different!
-G.Brooks

Clap your hands and stomp your feet; there's someone we'd like you to meet. She loves to hug and teaches to share.

What is her name?
Bubbie the Bear (x3)

Do you know what makes Bubbie's-Babies so great? It's the fact that they are all different! Join Bubbie the Bear and her gang as they learn to celebrate their differences and love the skin that they are in!

So, let the story begin by first looking at our friends as they run around and play outside. Then, at the end of the book, we'll stop and take a look at how my differences are applied.

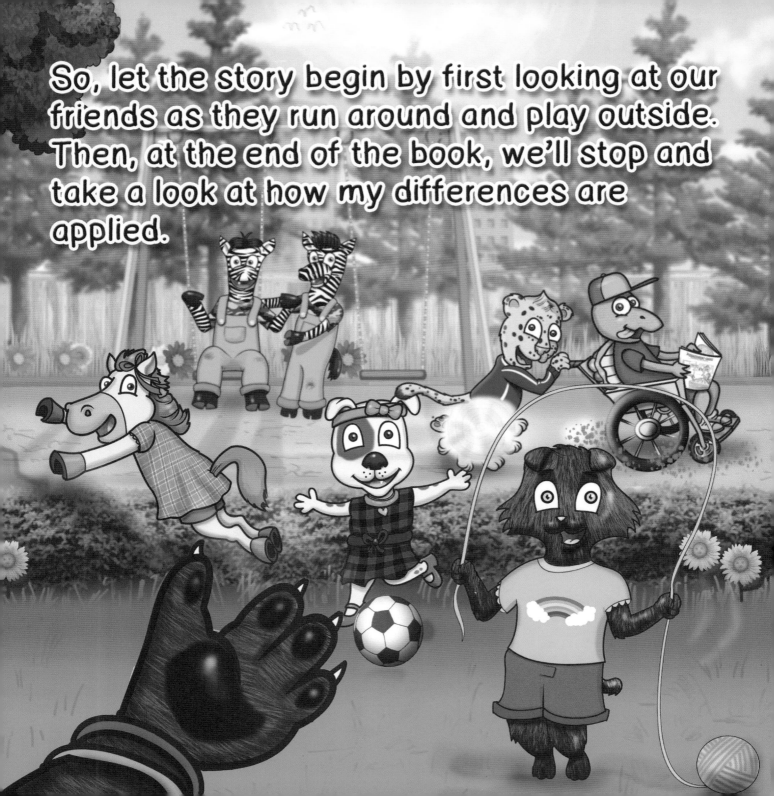

This is Leslie, a black cat; her ears lay very flat and, also, notice her short tail for it's these two special details which make her so cuddly and sweet!

Now, let's see who's over here. It's Michael and Lee, the Zebra pair, who at first glance might look the same, but have different eyes and different manes.

This is Teri, whose fur color may vary. See in the morning light, her fur color just might appear to be the color of light gray. But as the sun begins to go down, her fur color looks brown, which makes her different wouldn't you say?

Decker has spots and lines on his face and always loves to race around to see how fast he can run, but it's the traction on his feet which makes him a good athlete, and makes watching him play so much fun!

Now, where did Gio go? No one ever seems to know thanks to his ability to hide; since he can change the appearance of his skin you'll never know where he has been, making him difficult to be spied. Notice the glasses that he wears as they are a unique pair that covers the sides of his eyes.

Watch Piper as she gallops and jumps over a bush and gracefully flies through the air; her heart is so big that it makes up for the fact that she will never grow to the size of a full mare.

Shane the turtle has green skin and a shell upon his back, and he likes to relax in his wheelchair with a book upon his lap.

Don't forget Mr. Yakky, the art teacher, who's wacky and likes to wear his hair in different styles, but it's the clothing that he wears that will make you stop and stare and leaves all of the children laughing with a smile.

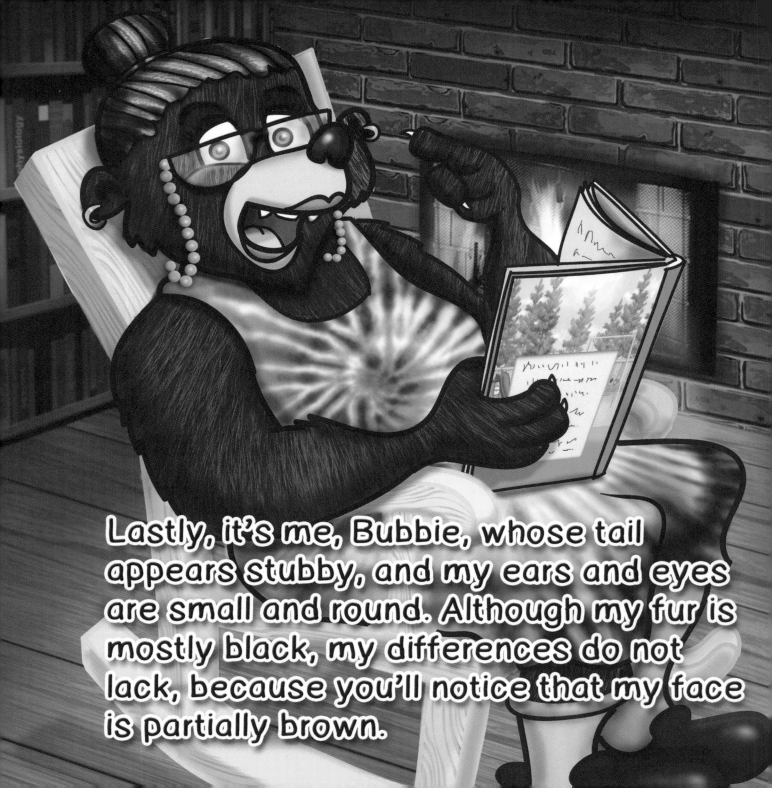

Lastly, it's me, Bubbie, whose tail appears stubby, and my ears and eyes are small and round. Although my fur is mostly black, my differences do not lack, because you'll notice that my face is partially brown.

Although we all look different, we all feel the same, that we should not be judged by our color or our eyes, or our manes, but instead by what we do and how we treat each other, because we feel that it's important to love one another!

And with that, the story's through, but always remember to be you, cause it's the little things you do that make you great! And always remember to be kind, because I'm sure that you will find that's it's our differences that we should celebrate!

ABOUT THE AUTHOR

Giovanni Brooks lives in a tree house and was the first man ever to befriend a black bear while hiking Mt. Everest (alternative facts)! He recently discovered his passion is writing stories—all of which are not true, this book is a prime example.

You might not have guessed this, but Giovanni is not Italian (gasp!) But is a black guy, with an Italian name, who was raised by his mother and her Jewish boyfriend. (Did you get all of that?) But wait there's more! He was raised with a Bubbie and Zayde (Yiddish for grandmother and grandfather respectively) and almost had a Bar Mitzvah when he turned 13 years old!

Growing up and attending College on the East Coast, he decided shortly after graduating to take a cross country road trip and relocate to San Diego. This ended up being the best decision of his life as it was here that he ultimately met his best friend turned wife and they now have two children!

HOW BUBBIES-BABIES WAS CREATED

While sitting in his home trying to come up with a name for his new Book series, Giovanni began to reminisce about him and his wife expecting their first child, and his mother explaining to him how she wanted her grandchild to refer to her as Bubbie... 2 years later he and his wife welcomed their second child and Bubbie now had her babies! Remembering the time that he spent with his Bubbie, and watching his children as they interact with their Bubbie, evoked feelings of love, warmth and happiness. He knew that these were the feelings that he wanted children to experience when reading his books. Result, Bubbies-Babies was thus created!

Beliefs: Bubbies-Babies believes that the future starts now. We focus on growing the best humans we can, while instilling values, morals, life lessons all while being wrapped up in a whimsical rhyming book! Bubbies-Babies icing on the cake, is that with the purchase of each book, a charitable donation will be made to various organizations!

Don't delay, educate your child and help an organization today!

Learn more about the Bubbies-Babies
series of books at Bubbies-Babies.com

WORD SEARCH

```
        S M E E L
      C G F E L R E S Q
    H T I Y I I A S H S Z
    Y D O O K B M H L A N C V
    P J T R K B S S I N V I G
  S P D E E A U H Z E E T O G E
  I A Q F K Y B E T E R I H H E
  Z H N O C F V P I O T P Y N J
  H X U G E E L I C I K I N D K
  L M L U D K Y P K Z Z V X V S
  M Z S E C N E R E F F I D
  Y S Q Y K W R F A M I L Y
  A A D V F R I E N D S
    H V R Q X I G N Y
        M E K I M
```

BUBBIE	HAPPY	SHANE
DECKER	KIND	SHARE
DIFFERENCES	LEE	SMILE
FAMILY	LESLIE	TERI
FRIENDS	MIKE	YAKKY
GIO	PIPER	

Congratulations

for being different!
You have just earned a "Bubbie Badge!"

B B

Bubbie
Badge

Please
color
me!